LET ME LIVE

ANSLEY ANDERSEN

BALBOA.
PRESS

A DIVISION OF HAY HOUSE

Balboa Press books may be ordered through booksellers or by contacting:

Balboa Press
A Division of Hay House
1663 Liberty Drive
Bloomington, IN 47403
www.balboapress.com.au
1 (877) 407-4847

Because of the dynamic nature of the Internet, any web addresses or links contained in this book may have changed since publication and may no longer be valid. The views expressed in this work are solely those of the author and do not necessarily reflect the views of the publisher, and the publisher hereby disclaims any responsibility for them.

The author of this book does not dispense medical advice or prescribe the use of any technique as a form of treatment for physical, emotional, or medical problems without the advice of a physician, either directly or indirectly. The intent of the author is only to offer information of a general nature to help you in your quest for emotional and spiritual well-being. In the event you use any of the information in this book for yourself, which is your constitutional right, the author and the publisher assume no responsibility for your actions.

Print information available on the last page.

ISBN: 978-1-5043-1556-2 (sc)
ISBN: 978-1-5043-1582-1 (e)

Balboa Press rev. date: 11/22/2018

CONTENTS

CONTENTS

CHARACTERS

Larsen Curtis	Barrister, wife
Osbourne Paton	Neurologist, husband
Tracey	Osbourne's Mum
Josephine	Victim ghost
Ramsey	Murderer
Gavin Wiley Book	Businessman
Rebecca	Gavin's daughter
Maggie	Josephine's sister
Alicia	Josephine's Mum
Joseph	Josephine's granddad
Anthony	Larsen's detective
Rebecca Thompson	Anthony's assistant
Germina Sage	Daughter
Hayden Salvator	Son

CHAPTER I

GLADNESS AND FREEDOM

I am walking down the road with my wife Larsen Gabrielle Curtis. We are heading home via public transport space vehicle at the time of this year 5102 in Sydney on the blue earth.

'Honey, you see over there.'

'Where?' I ask.

'Right there.'

'There, where? Where is there?'

'Oh my God!'

'Where is God?'

'You see, sweetheart. The old man across the street.'

'Oh! Yeah. What so funny?'

'He is talking to no one.'

'Really?'

'Of course.'

'You are a neurologist, Osborne. Do you understand what he is saying?'

'I'll try my best, baby.'

'Oh! Darling he crosses the road to come to this side.'

'Well! I will pay attention to what he is saying, babe, to be honest.'

After a while.

'What is the old man talking?'

'He is speaking............. speaking .... talking not in a concord manner ..... well I ....'

'Do you have any idea?'

'He is talking here and there. I pay more attention to his saying.'

'Any clue?'

'I think he is speaking about a lady.......... call Josephine or something like that.'

'Who is Josephine, then?'

'I am not Jesus, babe.'

'No idea?'

'No idea, at all.'

'Well! What are we doing now?'

'Here comes the space vehicle. Let's go on board, darling. Quick!'

'I am coming.'

On the other side of the earth there is a pair of lovers sitting at a table in a restaurant. They have just arrived and outside is heavy downfall. The lady is called Josephine Rebecca Thompson and the gentleman is called Ramsey Omega Riley. He is nicknamed RR. Simply because he works in a robot innovation firm which its core business is to manufacture new and advanced robots to do every day routines for human beings. They have been together for more than two years. Not co-habituate but lovers. On the surface! Why? The gentleman Ramsey is changing his heart towards Josephine. Well?

Six months ago, Ramsey went to Aston continent as business trip. Ramsey was sent by the Boss to persuade the wealthy man Gavin Wiley Book to purchase new robots from Ramsey's working firm Stewart Robots Innovations Enterprise. When Ramsey was at Gavin's office suite. Ramsey met Gavin's youngest daughter Rebecca. It is because Ramsey determined to pursue Rebecca as Gavin is a rich man in the continent. Gavin also has a business empire across the planet earth. It is Ramsey's ambition to grab Gavin's fortune as his own and then Ramsey will able to play ladies and to expend rigorously on this earth planet.

On the other hand, Josephine is a smart and good girl. She works in day time and study further in her career at evening classes in University. She is studying forensic science. This degree will enhance her archaeology career as a second core career in her life. She wakes up early in the morning and back home never after 1900 hours. Really, a good girl. No doubt about that!

Now they are having their dinner together. Josephine is talking happily and non-stop. Meanwhile Ramsey is having his problem. Ramsey's sensitive noses is blocking his breathing and he gradually out of air. Thus, Ramsey takes out the puffer to breathe. Gradually he is back to normal. Alternatively, back to monster's heart. Who knows?

'Darling, you look you have lost weight, haven't you?'

'Yeah! I work day and night these weeks. Besides my boss told me to complete a project then work out the promotion campaign in three week-time. Oh! My God. I am not your son. What am I able to do to complete this existing task?'

'What are you going to do then?'

'I have no idea, honestly. May be do my best or listen to the King's speech. Who knows?'

'You already have a weak body. Now you need to stay up late at night to work. It is a disastrous job.'

'What can I do, then? I cannot quit. Otherwise I have no cash to pay the bill and rent in cash. Tell, me then.'

'Anything I am able to help?'

'Yes, give me a kiss. That's enough, babe.'

'I am giving you now. Come on.'

They have a long kiss. Such a long time that both turn blush. My God!

They have this dinner for two hours. A long dinner that Josephine is going home late. The dinner is longer than the 'Battle of Waterloo', to be honest! Or shorter than a 'Galaxy War'. Who knows?'

Josephine is living with her younger sister named Maggie. Maggie is also a University student studying Philosophy and work as a part time guitar coach to earn some money to pay the fees and textbooks costs. These good girls stay, study and work in their early lives. They are living happily together without uttering a single word to show grief and pity. They both dream to a better life in the future and to have their own children and family and their dreamed paradise.

The two girls' father died soon after Maggie was born. Their mum is now on holiday and granddad is busy on his business affair. Mum is called Alicia and granddad is named Joseph. All four of them reside in the same apartment and everyone does his/her house work and four people prepare meals together. To cook their favourites and shared among them four. The 'Four Superiors'.

This day Wednesday March 23 my Mum Tracey comes back home happily. Mum has a weekend break to stay in a motel in the countryside. When Mum is home I set up her bedroom two days before her return. Together to get ready of any essential needed for Mum Tracey. Every time this happens my wife Larsen looks worry. Thus, I ask,

'Darling, are you right?'

'Not really!'

'I know but we both need to understand our own feelings.'

'What feelings?'

'Tracey is my Mum. After she married my dad. She suffered lots of nasty experiences. Before the marriage to my hypocrite dad my Mum was a happy girl. Many boys pursue Latrine. Dad used canny tricks to force Mum to the marriage party. Soon after they are married Mum had to wash the floor, clean the windows, cook the meals, wash the clothes and many more. Latrine works like a slavery dog. Meanwhile my dad just sits on the sofa to read his newspaper only and not bother to give a hand. Dad is a monster. He does not care about Mum and myself. He is worse than a termite wandering here and there but finally eaten by a cockroach.'

'You also need to know my feelings. I marry you but you only concern about your Mum. Not to utter any console inclination on my career and our own private life. If you were me what is your feeling?'

'Yes, I know. I promise to take care of you and my Mum. Besides, I really love you. I wish both of us to be good to Tracey. In return, I already am a good husband and be kind to your parents.

'We reside with Mum under the same roof. We cook, eat, chat, go out or family discussions together. We respect Mum's idea because she was considered as ignorant by dad when he was alive. Bastard! We respect Mum.

'After Mum goes to sleep at night. Both of us can work out what we need to do and then ask Mum's opinion to work together. I indeed wish to respect Mum. We have our suffering days and journey. I swear I will be a good son to take care of my Mum. Mum Tracey is the only blooded person I have in this world. I do not and pretty scare to lose her.

'Larsen, you are lucky. You were born in this continent inside FARE. You have not seen what is called poverty. What is suffering. You have everything since you were born. Not me and my Mum. I am not saying poverty is a suffering. But Mum and myself were being betrayed by our deadest family member and he is my dad. You do not have the feeling that being betrayed by a dad. Now he is dead. God!'

'But you and I need our own space.'

'Whenever Mum Tracey is residing with us. We are certain to

possess all the lucky relationships. Two heads are better than one head. Trust me.'

I continue, 'Larsen, three of us can live happily together and is better than only two of us. Whenever you become a mum you will understand. We can have children for Mum Tracey to educate. Larsen, no matter I have grown up or not. She is my Mum. I need her directions to become a good and talented man.'

'Osbourne, I know you are a good son. You still need to take me in consideration.'

'Yes, honey. I will do both. Good to Mum and you. Eventually we need to work together. If you do not understand my situation. Try to figure out my status.

'I listen to Mum and you. I always love my beautiful wife. Larsen, put yourself in my shoes. You are my wife. If I do not look after you. Who is going to do it? I don't wish any quarrels and disputes in our family. Whenever there is chaos we all need to sit down for a win/win solution.'

'I urgently need your love, Osbourne.'

'I will certainly give my love to you, Larsen my wife. Let's stay on track. I am good to my Mum and both of us are good to Mum. On our part, you will acknowledge I am a good son, a good husband and a good father. I am sure what you are thinking of. I promise to give all my love to Mum as a son and my wife as a husband. Okay?'

'I love you, Osbourne! I really do! Trust me.'

On the afternoon on the other day of a nasty day. God! I am going to have my lunch in a café close to Supreme Court of New South Wales. Today is different there are plenty of people waiting on a queue. No seats available and not a single gap you can squeeze in. No choice but to another café instead. It happens the same scenario. Last resort, go to the small café on Castlereagh Street. Not a day for me! Tough luck!

I sit on the table close to windows to look outside. The elderly, young adolescents and school children all walking together chatting and talking as they are walking along the road. What a great opportunity and beautiful scene out there. To my infancy I study hard and later get a part time job to finance my study and my Mum. We are the only two persons living on this blue earth. I don't mind. As fortunate as we both are happy without misfortunate omens. What can we say to Buddha and God?

The school years are only moments ago, lovely! At first, I am a lazy boy. Suddenly on one morning I tell myself I must study hard. Then I succeed to become top of the class. As I recall at that time some students are having an eye on me. Once the students are hurrying to hand in school work then leave. I give to the student in front of me with my hand wiping away the dirty rubbish on the book. Those students sitting next to me or in front of me smile and sigh. I have no idea what they are doing or thinking! Up to this day I am still in puzzle, not disengage this secret.

My lunch is coming I eat the garlic bread quickly as I am starving. Oh! no, the bread is bitter with trench smell. Also, the coffee is no good with an insect Gampoty floating on the top. I hurry pay the money and go back to my clinic which I purchase a cup of juicy drink for lunch. Today is not my day, mate!

Really an upset experience! What can I do? God sake! I am waiting for two patients to turn up in this afternoon. The appointment at 1500 hour is postponed to 1630 hour. No choice. After all consultations, I hurry home to cook dinner within 30 minutes to break the record.

While home Larsen is still in her office. I eat biscuits and drink a cup of orange tea plus tomato sandwiches. It is now 1800 hours Larsen is still not home. I then cook the dinner as I am waiting for my love to come back soon without delay. I wait until 1745 hour but Larsen is still out of my sight. I am hungry, frustrated and worry sitting on the lounge to watch television broadcast. Then a click on the lock and Larsen is back home. What a lovely moment!

'Where have you been, baby?'

'A party.'

'A party?'

'Yeah! A party.'

'What's that for?'

'I win an appeal case today. I decide to go to the hotel to have beer to celebrate with my colleagues.'

'Celebrate? You are pretty much lucky, baby. I am starving to death, but you celebrate?'

'Oh! I am sorry. Don't say this. Sweetheart.'

'Let's go to dinner straight away.'

'I love you!'

'I love you.'

CHAPTER 2

PATIENTS' ILLNESSES
AND SICKNESSES

Early next morning I stay at my home psychologist office waiting a patient. I sit on the sofa watching TV news. The presenter broadcasts several news of no interests to me. Then the news on a female ghost appears on the same spot at the same time every Thursdays at 2100 hours sharp from 28 days ago. The local suburban residents are talking about this matter for the last 10 days or so. News reporters interview the locals and are told they are very puzzled on the appearance of a ghost demon that is seemingly foolish. Then on the comments of a Buddha monk which he insists there are ghosts in this world. Who knows? No one person indeed really has seen a ghost up to this point. The ghosts are only happening in novels and films. Who cares! Actually, those locals really care and worry. Why? It is the only time a ghost appears in front of their homes. If you see a ghost, or something looks like a ghost walking here and there around the street where you are residing. It is scary, isn't it? Really! No lies, mate!

In the afternoon, I go to work in the Laboratory where I am the Managing Director and Founder, also Chairman of Board and Chief

Research Officer and Co-Founder of Advance Gene Therapy with Larsen. While I am busily looking information to the residence of Buddha and God. A team member from the Genetic Brain Research section comes in. He says,

'Brad, I am confused!'

'What confused?'

'I do not understand why people are still wondering where the outside signals come from?'

'What's wrong with it?'

'There is nothing wrong. We now all understand these messages are sent from other planets inside our Galaxy. Our Milky Galaxy is made up of 10 Planets which is universal truth. Why people in the 18ᵗʰ and 19ᵗʰ Centuries questioned these messages origin and determined to find out are there living organisms on other planets?'

'It is easy to answer this question.'

'What's the answer?'

'It is because they did not realise there are living creatures on the other side of this Galaxy.'

'Really?'

'Of course.'

'Really, I .... mean ....'

'Do you think the naughty boys and naughty girls decidedly send out messages to pretend these are coming from outer space?'

'Well! I ..... I ...... think ....'

'What do you think, then?'

'I think they are ......'

'They come to borrow medications from our Earth. It is a fact that happened more than 250 years ago. It was air on TV Computer and Radio Communications all over FARE.'

'Yes, I did watch the documentation.'

'What do you think now?'

'I think I better go to work.'

'Good on you, mate.'

On my research of brain functions inside all creatures in our Galaxy in comparisons with other Galaxy. I wonder, always wonder is there any connection among all of us? Is it originated from the same first living cell which spread to planet earth with the method and reason that is unknown to us at this time of the year? I wonder if? If I am correct. There is a connection among us all. Otherwise there will not have so many creatures living on different planets inside different Galaxy. These organisms and we human share the same origin but grow up under different circumstances and we still reproduce our own offspring in our environment. Days and nights. It is this that our brain functions are not the same but from the same beginning. Is it true? No one knows yet! Who knows?

When I am home. Mum Tracey and Larsen are waiting me for dinner. Tonight, Mum cooks my favourite food and Larsen has her own dish. All of us eat the dinner happily.

After dinner three of us sitting around to chat. Mum urges us to have a baby. Then, Larsen says quietly that she is having a baby now. What a surprise! It's amazing, Buddha and God! I am going to be a father. I can't wait. I am such happy that I cannot go to sleep that night. Next morning, I stay home to rest. Otherwise I make a wrong diagnose will harm my patient and cause problems. God!

After one day break it is time to commence work again. I am waiting in my home psychology clinic for a teenager to turn up. He is at the late teens and full of illusions inside his mind. He called me 10 days ago for a consultation. Now here he comes.

'Good morning Dr Osbourne!'

'Good day Robinson. What is your day?'

'Not really such good, really!'

'What's wrong?'

'I always have nightmares.'

'Of what?'

'I usually dream that I am staying on continent M106 on Planet Mars.'

'What for?'

'I watch news on Mars. It is to say Mars and Jupiter is going to collide in 145 day-time.'

'Really?'

'Absolutely! People on Mars and Jupiter are scary and flee.'

'What happens then?'

'My nightmare is up to right here and stop.'

'Isn't it to be continued next week?'

'Not really, Doc.'

'What's your feeling towards this dream?'

'I feel horrible.'

'Now you wake up?'

'Still terrified!'

'What's wrong with you, mate?'

'Is it to be coming true, Doc?'

'What's your opinion?'

'I dare not say.'

'What are you studying now?'

'Science degree in University.'

'Which degree?'

'Cosmology Diploma and mayor on astronomy advanced research.'

'Are you happy with your study?'

'Of course! I am, Doc.'

'Your academic results?'

'Excellent. Always High Distinction, honestly!'

'Besides study. What else do you do?'

'I sit at home to figure my career of what means to go to other further Galaxies.'

'Then?'

'Then I fall asleep.'

'I think you have thought a lot or indeed too much as required. It is no use to fancy of a great career without doing good preparation jobs before your career.'

'Then?'

'It is your illusion that causes your nightmare. But ...'

'Am I going to become crazy?'

'Absolutely not.'

'Thanks Buddha and God. Please have mercy on me!'

'What you need to do is not to daydream but actually work on your career. That is to study hard and planning your career of what is going to do to become successful.'

'That's it?'

'It is your decision.'

'But what?'

'I can prescribe a medication to ease or even cease your desire to daydream.'

'Then?'

'After 30 days of medication you are better off. No lies.'

'Really?'

'Definitely!'

'Thanks Doc. What should I thank you, Doc?'

'It is my job and I am doing my job. Only pay consultation fees and go free.'

'Thanks, bye!'

Besides this patient I have another 12 more patients coming today. What a day!

It is on a night Larsen has a horrible dream. Inside the dream is a female ghost talking to Larsen. The ghost says she is upset and annoy because of her fiancé Ramsey betrayed her and kill her by throwing her body into the ocean to feed huge whales and seagulls. The ghost tells all the happenings from onset to the end and begs Larsen to find justice and punish Ramsey to uphold righteousness.

When Larsen is awake the next morning. She forgets the story but the part to clear the ghost's name. The dream is so horrified that disturbs Larsen for a couple of days. This story matches the cell television news some time ago. Larsen is determined to do her best since she hates crimes to the highest level of human hatred and obsess with those crimes to cheat other people on family issues or commits offence and cheat money matters. These people cannot be forgiven and should be punished to the highest penalty.

There is a student patient coming to my consultation clinic later in the afternoon. Before this I have nothing to do but hanging around. When the girl comes, she says,

'Doctor, I always fail in my tests and examinations. It is my college counsellor urges me to a psychology consultation.'

'Anna, do you understand why you always fail?'

'Honestly, I have no idea.'

'Do you prepare for your examinations?'

'Of course, I do!'

'Why you finally fail?'

'I suppose I do not memorise the whole lot.'

'You memorise the whole lot?'

'Yeah!'

'Yeah?'

'What's the problem?'

'There is a big problem.'

'What's that?'

'You can't memorise the whole book and go to sit for your examinations, to be honest!'

'Why? What is the reason?'

'You need to understand what is taught from your High School teachers and write it on the answer sheets.'

'Really?'

'Not really!'

'What's the point?'

'Besides, do you take notes on your own?'

'Yes, I do.'

'What's your notes?'

'I summarise the book and put it into short notes.'

'You are certain to fail.'

'Why?'

'No one can memorise all textbooks in his/her such many years of study.'

'Why?'

'I don't know why. It is learnt from my University Lecturers.'

'Then?'

'Then what?'

'I have lots of time to read my textbooks.'

'You'd better look before you leap.'

'What's wrong with it?"

'There is nothing wrong.'

'The point is…?'

'Everyone has his/her own type of procedure to study. It is that fashion will help you to go to success or not.'

'Well! You mean my style is not correct?'

'You need to work out your style before it is too late, Anne.'

'I will. Thanks Doc.'

'Any questions?'

'No further questions!'

'Bye then.'

'Bye Doc.'

This guy is really a silly girl. Her academic results are not good as others and she does not know what to do. Goodness me! What a day!

Regarding the ghost case. Larsen calls me to tell me what she has found so far! Here is her story.

'Darling, I got a new cue. It is found that Josephine's private helicopter vehicle was once someone had set the vehicle computer to go to a place and then back to one more place after this. It is found by my detective Anthony and his partner Rebecca Thompson.

'Anthony is a PhD on Advanced computerised technology. He is double majors on Special Design and Manufacturing. Anthony finds the computer system is blocked by an external wave for a while and then flew to a park which is St. Holy Emperor's Park situated on the northern island. After this the helicopter was flying to a remote beach on the other side of the island.

'The question is who set the schedule and why it is going to a Park and then to a beach? This doesn't bother Anthony because they find out there are witnesses on the Park who really did see Josephine inside the helicopter but no one else. Rebecca deduces that first on a park then a beach. It is because the beach is famous for its whale season and rough sea waves for the surfers on vacations. Then it is Josephine's turn to be murdered by a murderer who is the suspect Ramsey.

'Anthony also finds out Ramsey is a Master Degree on Advanced Computerised Technology which he gets a credit pass. During his study, his classmates all say he is obliged by the Lecturer to stop disturbing female students while in lecture and was warned two times from University Officials.

'It is presumed Ramsey pre-set the vehicle and killed Josephine on the beach and flew her to the ocean to feed the whales for dinner. The problem is we do not have witnesses and we cannot prove this evidence on court. It is simply Ramsey can argue that there are plenty of computer undergraduates. It does not mean it is Ramsey to kill Josephine.

'Rebecca has gone to the Roman Empire Beach to look for more fatal evidences and other related proofs but Anthony comments that it is only a glim of hope. No surprise success.'

Nowadays students in University have to study up to at least a Master Degree to look for a job. Otherwise people cannot find any job without the Master Certificate. The wages are far more than sufficient for us to pay all expenses and everyone has spare money to spend on other nonsense luxurious commodities as to enjoy a lovely luxurious life to show off.

After one week of the teenager consultation, this afternoon is free. I turn on the TV computer to watch the documentary showing the inside earth is still, but less, roaring under fire. Why? It is because scientists have deduced an operation to lower the temperature inside the earth crust. What method? They learn from the experience of our Planet Earth at the beginning of the Big Bang. At that time, the earth cooled down to a solid earth. This is what scientists have induced and deduced to repeat the experience to lower the temperature beneath the crust. What are they doing? They are doing a good job!

Today's weather is pretty much hotter than yesterday. It is in its high 30s. Hence, I switch on my mini-air-conditioner on the button at the left side of my computer glasses to get a cool day. What a day, mate!

On Planet Armstrong, Ramsey is teaching university students on a diploma of computer. Many students realise Ramsey is a bad man and try to humiliate Ramsey.

'Lecturer, what's wrong with the idea to manufacture robots to help we humans to do our jobs which is to let us to have more leisure time to spare?'

'It is no use to do that. The reason is people get lazy and not to work hard.'

'Everybody works on the planet anywhere of the Galaxy. No one is lazy.'

'It is what you think.'

'it is correct, isn't it?'

'It is not. At first stage people are still hardworking. Later then, they leave work to robots to have a KitKit and talk to one another. Gradually, they are lazy people not willing to work anymore.'

'It sounds good?'

'It looks good, doesn't it?'

'They may be lazy but not everyone?'

'They may be but not myself.'

This is the conversation among students and Ramsey. All Ramsey said are good points and no error. It is Ramsey's ugly face that he does not show his real poisonous face to let people know. He pretends to be good and a good man to work hard. Look at that! He only studied up to Master Degree and stops his academic career to work. Why to work, then? To earn money. What for? To play girls! Before anyone Ramsey is a good person who does not do any single thing wrong and to remind himself on this. Really? Only Buddha and God know! Why they know? Ask them yourself!

CHAPTER 3

LIFE OR DEATH

The ghost case happens when Larsen dreamt the ghost on a night. Larsen was horrified and worried the following day to lose mood on work. After a few days rest and deep thinking and feels stronger. Larsen returns to normal shape. Maybe even better than before.

After the dream Larsen is determined to accept this case and bring justice to Josephine as to punish Ramsey. Hence, Josephine is waiting and waiting. Waiting what? Waiting to dream the female ghost again on a night. Fortunately, Larsen finds nothing. But she is still waiting. My goodness!

The private female detective Rebecca Thompson reports to Larsen that she has found a couple of people had really seen Ramsey and Josephine on the night of murder. Everyone said they looked perfect and glad on that night without any quarrel. After a while Josephine drive her helicopter flying away and Ramsey departed on himself. Every incident is quiet and harmonious. Nothing went wrong. Now why is Josephine getting missing suddenly and she is gone to become a ghost appears inside Larsen's dream?

In my home-sited psychology clinic. This patient says,

'Doctor, I always fantasise I am a smart person. Every girl loves me. I am able to do everything to perfect.'

'When did you first have got this delusion?'

'Almost 15 months ago from now.'

'Does it bother you?'

'Not really! But ….'

'What?'

'Sometimes it comes robust that I cannot stop this fancy up to the time I go to sleep.'

'Then?'

'Then what?'

'Afterwards, what are you doing?'

'I resume to my work and study.'

'Afterwards?'

'I feel much better.'

'Why?'

'I feel glad and I love these dreams, Doc.'

'You love it?'

'Of course, I do, Doc.'

'Robert, you are a student, aren't you?'

'Yes, I am.'

'Do you feel more pressure or anyone is pushing hard on you?'

'Not really.'

'What is really, then?'

'My dad always wants me to become the first in class.'

'Then?'

'He urges me to keep studying day and night.'

'Do you have any recreations afterwards?'

'No.'

'No going out nor any sport?'

'None!'

'Do you enjoy your school work?'

'Absolutely!'

'Now, Robert. What I am going to do is to give you medication to relax yourself. You take morning and evening doses with one tablet each time.'

'And then?'

'And then you are becoming better now.'

'Thanks, Doc.'

'Okay, see you on the street.'

'Thanks Doc. Bye.'

Returning to the puzzle of the roaring fire inside our Planet Earth. There is a proposal in the 32nd Century that at that time the astronomers, physicists and philosophy theorists launched a theory of why the fire inside the ball is still burning! They explained it is at the time of Big Bang then the Earth cooled down. At that moment, inside the ball is continuing to be hot. It stays there up to nowadays. Why it cools down?

Look at a burning building. It starts to burn suddenly and goes on and on. The area becomes pretty much hot. When firemen and firewomen extinguish the fire. We can see the smoke rising. The theorists induce that the smoky mist appears is because of the cold stuff of the burnt building reacts with the outside air which is cold. At least, colder than the burning premise. Thus, there are smoky mist.

It means the same to Big Bang. After the explosion, the earth was a ball of fire. Then there is the earth crust separates the earth and the outsider. It is why there is a crust and later becomes oceans and land on Earth Planet. The Earth abruptly cools down is the fire ball already departed from that big mass which is even much hotter than the Earth.

Now the Earth is off the hot air which makes the Earth cools down suddenly. Do you believe in it?

Why the inside is still burning? It is the insider is retaining the hot air with high temperature without escaping to outside. Alternatively, there are eruptions of volcanoes. After this happening, there are plants then animals and then human being appear on Earth. It's a puzzle.

This theory is still debating. Why some object but some agree? No one knows! Those agree and disagree work in collaboration to decrease the temperature inside the ball successfully as mentioned on TV Computers and News Computers. Are they serious? Of what? They do not believe in this theory but they are able to alleviate the inside temperature. Is it luck? I have no idea! Better ask those scientists yourself. Don't bother me, mate! Miracle indeed! Take your turn, mate! Be careful! Look before you leap! Thanks Buddha and God. May they have mercy on us!

CHAPTER 4

✛

BUSY OR LEISURE

Larsen is busy on her other two cases of fraud and defamation. The cheating case is among three people and two big organisations which all are situated on FACE. The defendants deceive commercial information to sell to a smaller firm by telling the organisation the material is confidential which is saved in a secure disk. Indeed, they sold it for huge amount of money.

The other case is a lady suddenly quarrel with her office colleague and he condemn her as a whale beach. She is annoyed and determined to sue the guy with all the best possible she could. Larsen is also expecting the unexpected!

Today is 29 November, 5013. A Saturday sultry afternoon with occasional showers as reported by weather forecast. After lunch three of us go to a Park to watch other people walking, talking and children playing inside the Park. Mum Tracey urges Larsen to have more babies which Larsen smiling to say she will. My goodness! Many babies! I need to rent or purchase a bigger apartment to retain my family all together under a safe same roof. My God! My God!

In the blue sky, there are helicopters flying all around. Mostly are delivery vehicles to bring food, furniture or vehicles to customers and homes. Close to the Park, there is a restaurant nearby. Currently, it is pretty much hard to run this type of business. People are purchasing food from supermarkets or other food outlets or wholesalers to deliver to their home apartments. These food is delicious and tasteful without doubt. Hence, less people are going out for dinner.

Such restaurants are doing business at breakfast and lunch time which is their favourite hours. At this time office workers go for a sip of coffee in the morning or afternoon tea before returning home. Some have breakfast and lunch inside the restaurants. These patrons are mostly from other Galaxies. Thus, the chef needs to prepare their home food together with delicious food on FARE. What a great job, mate! Sometimes Earth residents also visit these restaurants. They usually go there on birthday party or have meals with friends. Therefore, not much business at dinner time. Goodness me!

On Tuesday while I am inside my Lab office. Two members of the team on Advanced Galaxy Research come in.

'Hi.' Member one says.

'How are you going, mates!'

'Osbourne, I got a problem.'

'What's that?'

'I wish to research a successful mean to rescue a planet which is in danger.'

'What?'

'Yes, we are thinking a schedule to process the way to save a damaging planet.' Member two says.

'Good idea, indeed!'

'The problem is it is a first time to do this type of job.'

'Yes, the problem is what?'

25

'We do not have sufficient material to show us what to do.'

'That's a problem.'

'We can only look for them from secondary data which are not detailed and helpful.'

'Please go on.'

'What we are thinking is we need to travel to Planet #58 on Galaxy #2088 to see what's going on there.'

'Why?'

'Their planet is having problems.'

'What's in turmoil?'

'The land is pretty much harder and harder such they are not able to grow crops nor even grass to feed the animals.'

'This is a problem.'

'What do you think, Osbourne?'

'What is your solution?'

'We need to be there as quick as possible before it is too late.'

'God!'

'God is saying we need to give them a hand.'

'Goodness me!'

'Their culture and technology are backward to the same as Earth in the 12th Century.'

'Jesus!'

'Jesus is coming back in a short time, mate.'

'Dear me!'

'We have to do it quick as to target to save the planet.'

'What's the mean?'

'We go there to find out all essential information and to figure a good implementation to overcome it.'

'Jesus!'

'We are ready to go. It can be done by tomorrow 2:30pm Sydney time.'

'Then?'

'Then we come back hoping to have some good news, mate!'

'Good on you, then!'

'Thanks Osbourne, thanks.'

'My pleasure, mate.'

Regarding these Galaxies we are now inside it. There were many rumours in the 12th to 26th Centuries on Earth about Unidentified Flying Objects (UFO). Humans are suspecting there are other living organisms on other side of the Galaxy. Humans go to research to look for these, may be dangerous aliens, all the time. Goodness! Are the messages sent by boys and girls on Earth? Are they naughty enough to create these false messages to disturb scientists at that period of timeframe? Nonsense! It is certain to have intellectual organisms round there. The fact is the people of that period do not have sufficient information and technology to work out their existences to contact and talk to them. Hoping a Peace Contract!

CHAPTER 5

✛

PROFESSIONAL OR NON-PROFESSIONAL

I am busily on my own research of genetic study while my University class-mate turns up suddenly.

'Hi Osbourne, how are you going?'

'I am Okay! And you?'

'Pretty good, hopefully.'

'Osbourne, I am researching on the organ functions of those people living on Planets P26 and Q508.'

'That's really good. What have you found, Michael?'

'I have no idea. I am in a mess, honestly.'

'What's happening?'

'I found out they are functioning in a different way in response to our human physiology.'

'Really?'

'Not really!'

'What followed?'

'I wish to look for a way to cure their diseases without much of using medication.'

'Sounds good! And then?'

'I can't get any cue, to be honest!'

'Mike, there are scientists studying in the implementation of self-controlled identification to heal diseases we currently are having.'

'Really, Osbourne?'

'Absolutely, Michael!'

'What is their findings?'

'They have no cure yet at this moment.'

'What happens?'

'They are now treating patients with some other means.'

'What means?'

'By exercise.'

'Jesus!'

'Jesus is at your back!'

'What exercise then?'

'To do soft exercise that leads to self-recovered.'

'Amazing!'

'A man is sinking!'

'Then?'

'This is all they can do currently.'

'What's the progress of their research to recover by self-immune system?'

'Only a bit of not vital clues yet.'

'Stupid!'

'Exactly!'

'What about the other method on exercising to return to normal?'

'A great success, Mike!'

'Okay, Osbourne. I need to go back to my lab. See you later!'

'Thanks, bye!'

He leaves as quick as disappearance of a morning dew. God!

Now I am home from work. Mum and Larsen are cooking dinner together. I hurry to give them a hand after dropping off my summer chilly shirt which keeps me cool all through my body without turning on my personal air-conditioner under the sun light. Three of us are talking to one another while cooking the meal. Then all of us sit down to enjoy what we have cooked. Oh! Cook or Cooker?

After dinner, our night is pretty much quiet that three of us start to read books from our computer lenses. Mum is reading history from the onset of Human Beings on earth up to now the FACE. Larsen is reading legal theory books regarding to reform legal system on other planets. I am reading a documentary journal on cosmology. Larsen is already three-month pregnant. She looks extraordinary perfect. Her body shape has changed but still looks not too heavy with the baby inside. She works during the day and come back home to cook meals. Seems nothing has happened. My goodness!

What the editor of the journal is saying that in 29th century, some cosmologists and astronomers are debating on the concept of whether there are 3,000 Galaxies inside our Space. Some argue it is while some say may be more. Who is right?

They also argue that when does time start to count its minutes? Some say that we need to look for the oldest Galaxy in our Space to check the age of that Galaxy. By this we are capable to realise when the time commence. Where is the oldest Galaxy? Look for it!

Is our Milky Galaxy the oldest or youngest Galaxy? If Not! Where is the oldest Galaxy? Are there still some new Galaxy are forming its shape somewhere on the other side of our Space?

To constitute a Galaxy is an easy job. Only gathering the cloud and sand on Space to row them together. Then until it is pretty much hot and then it explodes to form new planets. God's miracle! Trust me! The question is what is the length of this episode to take to form a new

Galaxy? Ten billion years or one hundred billion years or even pretty much longer? Ask God, mate!

The astronomers were debating this controversy for more than 200 years. Until 31st century cosmologists are having the first evidence on other existing Galaxies in Space. From that time onwards, there are more and more new evidences to say it is only 3,000 Galaxies. Up to now the 52nd century we still are looking for these 3,000 Galaxies besides we only have found 250 Galaxies in total. Who is right? God or yourself? Jesus, why don't you come back the second time? What is going to be written on this article will be waiting until part II next month.

Regarding the ghost case, Larsen has decided to take up this mysterious case to take the challenge. To tell the world or Galaxies that what is correct and what is dirty wrong. Recently, there are sayings that the murderer Ramsey is spreading the rumour that his girlfriend the ghost Josephine, deserts him to run away with another man to other planets. God! What is he doing? Goodness me! Is he under any spiritual influence? Is he sane or not close to sane? Is he an animal? He is worse than a rat, Jesus! Jesus, please have mercy on we humans and come back the second time, thanks!

Larsen is determined to clear the name of the ghost. It means to punish Ramsey this monster. No matter there is not much hope and no matter it is further and further away. Larsen is decisively to do it. Once and for all! God, why we humans always suffer so many misfortunes and disasters on this planet earth?

In the morning, a patient is waiting in my restroom inside my home clinic waiting to be served.

'Doctor Osbourne, I always have a strange dream.'

'What's that, Sawyer?'

'I dream that Jesus is talking to me.'

'Really?'

'Absolutely!'

'Jesus Christ!'

'He is talking to me face to face.'

'What does he say, then?'

'He tells me he is coming back to earth may be the second time.'

'Oh! Jesus, really?'

'I have no idea, Doc.'

'What idea do you have, Sawyer?'

'Is my dream fuzzy?'

'If it is true. It is a good dream, frankly.'

'What do you think, Doc?'

'Well! I ....'

'I think the dream makes no sense.'

'This is a possibility. My idea is you go back home to see the dream is coming back or not. If it is not, then you are fine. If yes you are, in my opinion, in deep trouble.'

'Okay! Thanks Doc.'

'See you.'

'Bye Doc.'

CHAPTER 6

CASES AND CASES

Regarding the ghost's case Larsen is pretty much upset from onset until present. Larsen is such annoyed that she always hates those men to desert their wife or partner and turn to another girl. That girl maybe more beautiful or much wealthier than his old partner. God sake dam it! Honestly, Larsen is now 5-month pregnant. She wishes to concentrate on this ghost case. It is why Larsen leaves behind other cases to her staff barristers to deal with as to accomplish to focus on this mysterious ghost case. But Larsen is having a big belly to walk in difficulty. Larsen insists she is fine and keep moving. Almighty God! Gosh!

At present time of 1450 hours Larsen has some new threads from Rebecca Thompson while I am in my Lab. Rebecca tells Larsen on the night of murder, there are witnesses to prove Ramsey was sitting inside the park to talk with other elders for a long period of time. Many elders are willing to tell this fact to certify each other's affidavit to be right. My goodness! What method was implemented to kill Josephine? As Ramsey was not at the murder site nor on the helicopter vehicle. Did Ramsey kill Josephine from a remote control? Goodness me, Lord!

Inside my Lab office the other Professor from the Robinson Advanced Genetic Research Association suddenly turns up.

'Hi, Osbourne. How are you going?'

'I am OK! What about you, Stuart?'

'Pretty good at this time.'

'That's good. Good news, frankly!'

'My team is looking for any procedure totally to alter we human DNA as to build a strong mankind to appear inside this big Space.'

'What for, Stuart?'

'To build a new mankind that all people are intelligent and kind-hearted.'

'Are you kidding?'

'I am not keating, mate!'

'What's your opinion?'

'I think it is a good manner to give a go.'

'Go for what?'

'Go for gold!'

'Any report?'

'Not at this point, to be honest.'

'What are you going to do then?'

'Honestly, my team is undergoing several schedules to look for new devices, but ......'

'But what?'

'No luck!'

'Really?'

'Absolutely!'

'Oh! Gosh! Why I was born in this century?'

'I am attempting to get more information and interpretations on this matter. At the end, no luck!'

'What are you going to do then?'

'My team of genetic scientists are having no beads on this issue. We are in a mess. We are inside the mist and lose our way to go out.'

'Horrible, isn't it?'

'Extremely pitiful!'

'Then?'

'Then ...... What then? .... Then ....'

'Then what's your next step?'

'We have no idea!'

'Not even a perfect thing?'

'Shamefully, it is not!'

'What are you going to do now?'

'I wish to work out more techniques to see what we are capable to do.'

'Good on you, mate!'

'Oh! I have to go.'

'Why? In such a rush?'

'My wife is waiting to dine with me tonight.'

'Oh! Jesus, why do you come back at such a late date?'

'My wife tells me to hurry home as soon as I am able to.'

'Enjoy your dinner!'

'Thanks. Bye!'

'See you later!'

After dinner I am reading a novel inside bedroom. I've suddenly got an idea. I speak to Larsen.

'Honey, do you love me?'

'Of course, I do! What a silly question!'

'If I have a girl outside. What is your response at that time?'

'I am certain to divorce you.'

'Really?'

'Exactly.'

'This is your reaction to what I just said?'

'Yes, for sure!'

'Are you annoy then.'

'No, I am not.'

'Why?'

'Because you have changed your heart. There is no way to turn back.'

'Then?'

'Just let it goes!'

'Do you upset?'

'Of course, no!'

'Why?'

'It's all because you are a bad boy.'

'I ain't, Sweetie!'

'Yes, you are.'

'Any other options?'

'Not really!'

'Shall we sit down and talk?'

'What for?'

'Conciliation.'

'No need to do that!'

'Why is that no need?'

'No need to change a naughty boy's mind.'

'Oh! God. Please have mercy on me. Please!'

'God won't help you, Honey.'

'Why? I am a good husband!'

'No, you are not. Definitely.'

'No, I am a perfect husband!'

'I am certain to leave you whenever you have a mistress.'

'Sure?'

'Pretty sure!'

'Where are you going to, then?'

'I have lots of places to travel to. This is none of your business.'

'At that time, I am not a naughty boy but a pity boy!'

'You deserved it!'

'Baby, if I changed my mind to come back to you. What's your feeling?'

'I won't accept you again.'

'Are you sure?'

'Pretty sure!'

'Let's have sex now! Sweetie!'

'Our baby girl was just born three weeks ago.'

'Let's make it.'

'Why?'

'My drive is excited!'

'Oh! Funking man!'

'Let's do it now. Honey. Let's do it!'

'Oh! Funk, funk!'

More than 30 days are elapsed. All three of us are busy. Mum is busy on her home business. Larsen is going to her legal office as usual. I am busy on my clinic and research. Pretty busy! Who is looking after our baby daughter Germina, naked name Prudence? No one! Are you keating? Who cares? Fortunately, Prudence cried in recent nights. Larsen and myself woke up in the mid-night to take care of Prudence. Lord! Both of us are fatigue the following day. Specially Larsen as after her postpartum still needs more sleep and sufficient energy.

While we are on bed inside our bedroom. I commence to say,

'Baby, are you Okay on your daily work?'

'Not really!'

'Are you sure?'

'Not the first couple of days but yesterday.'

'You need more rest indeed.'

'Yes, of course.'

'We both take turns to look after Prudence. I do it in the mornings and you are in afternoons.'

'Alright!'

'You also need to take care of your body. Don't overworked yourself.'

'Thanks, sweetie.'

'From now on no matter big or small matters. We discuss it then come to a solution. No quarrels, right?'

'Pretty sure!'

'You look really great tonight!'

'Am I?'

'Perfect!'

'Sure?'

'Let's have sex now!'

'Oh! God!'

'God is saying 'Yes', honey!'

'You Funking,……….. Funking you!'

'Yes, I am doing a man's job.'

'Oh! My God! Oh…….'

'Yes …….. yes baby!'

'Funk …….. funking you!'

Another three months have elapsed. Our Prudence is cooing and has her rooting reflex whenever she sees Larsen. All four of us in the family are happy. No doubt about that! Absolutely!

Fortunately, my brain cells research comes to a halt. I am stuck on the question on what methods do they automatically repair themselves on their own without outside aids. It is known long ago the neurons are working together to form any images we see or sounds we hear.

These stimuli come and go to every part of our human brain to form a picture. Same as to watch a in cinemas in 26th century. Same as the cameras produced in 23rd century. They work the same way but different apparatus. But which neuron is responsible for which part of the job is indeed interesting and demands explanations on the puzzles! God, please have mercy on me to get over it! As soon as possible, please, God! Thanks, God! Where is God, then? Don't ask me! Still under research, honestly!

Do the neurons repair themselves as predicted by scientists on the process of plasticity in the 23rd century? If "Yes"! What is their means to do the job? They can form a picture in front of us to watch the scenery inside this Milky Galaxy and beyond. To watch every motion of anything on land or at the bottom of the ocean. Once they are impaired. The methods they implement to repair and save themselves are indeed challenging. Really? Exactly! My noble Lord!

CHAPTER 7

A New Born

ur baby girl Prudence is six months old. A sudden coming and a gradual growing. She is capable to response to Mum's smiles, Larsen's kisses and whenever I touch her cheek. She is giving back her rooting reflex. Prudence is now trying to say single word. She is fantastic to learn to speak in only six months old. Lord! Prudence says "Gae Mi" to Mum Tracey. Says "Mur Mur" to Larsen and to me is "Bed Bed". I can't believe it. Really? Don't believe it then!

On Larsen's ghost case, there are some new threads to consider. On the night of murder, Josephine's vehicle is, as said before, set down to fly to the beach automatically on its own. No matter what manual operation or re-set is no use. It was all set on that very particular morning, according to Anthony. Who set it? It is a puzzle.

In the morning Ramsey was busy on video conference with a client on issue of expending more capital in that organisation as investment. In the afternoon Ramsey was on hot debate with his supervisors on promoting the robot business by research on robot industry in the coming century. And to occupy a larger market share. They argued for more than two hours and a half and came to no solution. Later then, in the afternoon Ramsey was inside his office with two other colleagues preparing for the business trip to Planet Q66P1 to invest on their mechanics industry which is an infant industry for that planet and the local administration is eager to step up the pace to the mature stage on business cycle.

Hence, there is no evidence so far to suspect Ramsey is the person who set the automation on Josephine's helicopter computing vehicle. Who did it?

In the afternoon while I am struggling on my brain research with frustration inside my Lab office. Suddenly a guy turns up. He is my class-mate in University. Both of us always talk in lectures that resulted by expulsion to outside of the lecture theatre. Jesus! Alfred is now a Professor in advance brain technology and is doing his research in a large organisation with good reputation both the organisation and himself.

Alfred says, 'Osbourne, not seen you for a while. How are you going?'

'I am Okay! And you?'

'I am alright. Still 1.68 metres tall as before.'

'You look great, indeed.'

'Really?'

'Absolutely!'

'What's your progress on brain research?'

'It comes to something to stir up a mental contest.'

'What for?'

'For nothing. For stupidity! Simple!'

'My research is now mainly concerned with human or living organism's conversation.'

'And what?'

'To talk via brain signals.'

'Oh! Really?'

'Exactly!'

'What is the process?'

'We are still on the act of war, same as you.'

'What war?'

'Do you think it is a good idea?'

'Of course, why not?'

'In the preceding centuries people talk by exchange brain signals is only found in science fictions.'

'Yes.'

'My idea is what means is able to let the signals travel to the other brain in an instance?'

'Maybe velocity of light! What's wrong?'

'We already know our own brain signals is moving with the same speed of light to reach its target cells. It is only inside the body. Not going out of mind, honestly.'

'What's the difference?'

'The difference is will these signals do its job in the same way as inside our body to travel to the other side of the brain?'

'Maybe, why not?'

'The problem is "Why"?'

'Why?'

'I don't know why!'

'Good reply!'

'Maybe you need more work on your brain.'

'Maybe and maybe not. I have no idea to be honest.'

'You will do it. You are smart, mate!'

'What's your opinion, Osbourne?'

'I never come up with this topic, frankly.'

'Now I am telling you this.'

'I have no idea where to begin. Simply it is quite a new idea, mate!'

'What's your brain research going?'

'Going good.'

'What are you doing now?'

'I am currently on the work of improving brain cell functions disregarding the implementation of DNA.'

'DNA is good indeed, mate!'

'Yes, it is. I am on the research to promote brain cell function whenever they are going to be useless to return to their peak function. By this, I am trying to promote the functions to a better shape while an infant is born with brain damage of whatever reasons with DNA abnormal functions.'

'It is great!'

'It is a great loss!'

'Don't despise yourself, Osbourne please!'

'I am not keating!'

'What's the concern?'

'I honestly not able to figure it out.'

'Really?'

'Definitely!'

'It takes time to be honest.'

'It really and actually takes lots of time!'

'Okay, I got to go. My Mum and my wife are waiting me to a Museum to see the clothe which Jesus was putting on when he was on the cross.'

'Where?'

'It was found long ago in the 20th century and it is now an artefact to show Jesus' presence at that time.'

'Absolutely!'

'Okay, have a good day. It is good to talk to you.'

'I learn a lot from you every time.'

'Okay, bye'

'See you later!'

At this time of the year human beings may say we are fortunate or unfortunate. It all depends on what you feel and see. You are feeling good then it is good. Otherwise it is bad. All our daily essentials are supplied by the Planet Government. Our furniture, clothes, study, transportation or communication, all these are provided by Government. They place all commodities inside Government stores for sale. We citizens only pay a small sum of cash to purchase. The delivery is free of charge and services are polite and courtesy.

These products are designed by our Planer designers who completed Master Degree on Design Courses. They work for the Planet. Repaying the debt to the Planet. It is why we see everyone is putting on the same style of clothes or furniture or same helicopter vehicles but of different colours and other differentiations and in the same idea. Gosh!

In the morning I have three patients coming to my psychology clinic and only one in the afternoon. The boy is named Antonio and his father Alfred.

'Good morning, Doctor!'

'Come on in.'

'Thanks.'

'Please take a seat.'

'Here we are!'

'What's the problem?'

'My son always pronounces he is the greatest Philosopher ever existing on the Planet.'

'Really?'

'Yeah, exactly.'

'What's your concern?'

'I think he is having problems inside his brain or damages in his brain neurons.'

'Maybe or maybe not.'

'Could you please do something about it, Doc?'

'Of course, I will.'

'Son, please tell the doctor what you feel and sense of this world.'

'I am the finest philosopher ever on this Planet! I really am, no doubt about it!'

'What makes you to get this idea?'

'It is universal true, honestly!'

'What truth is that?'

'I am a student in philosophy class in University. I do all assessments with creative ideas.'

'Is it?'

'Of course, it is, frankly!'

'Your Lecturers told you this?'

'No, they don't.'

'What method that makes you think you are the best?'

'I have great ideas. I also figure there are many gods in Heaven. Not only our Holy God and Jesus Christ live in the Heaven above us.'

'There are many gods?'

'Yeah!'

'The Bible only says there is only one God in Heaven. You are now saying there are many gods in Heaven. Do you have a second thought on this?'

'I don't need any second thought. It comes from my sixth sense.'

'Are you kidding?'

'I am not keating, to be honest.'

'Where are the other gods, then?'

'They travel wherever they like and eat whenever they wish.'

'Leisure lives!'

'This is their daily style.'

'When did you come up with this idea?'

'When I was a teenager.'

'How old are you now?'

'I am 27 years old and going to be 28 on the fifth of next month.'

'Are you married?'

'Divorce!'

'The reasons?'

'My wife considers me as a ridiculous being.'

'What did she say about you?'

'She said I am in a position of only minding myself and always feel I am the greatest.'

'Your response?'

'I ignore her ugly criticisms.'

'Then?'

'Divorce.'

'When did that happen?'

'Five years ago.'

'You married at an early age?'

'Of course, why not?'

'Then divorce?'

'Yeah!'

'Why do you get married in the first instance?'

'I need a wife.'

'What for?'

'To clean the apartment and manage the daily routines and look after our children.'

'Like a slave?'

'Not a slave. It is her job.'

'Your job?'

'To work on my philosophical theories.'

'Any other paradigms besides the theory of many gods existing?'

'Not at this moment, unfortunately!'

'After divorce, you stay alone?'

'Yeah!'

'What do you do?'

'On my philosophy.'

'Any others?'

'Not at this moment for the time being.'

'You have nothing to create but telling there are many gods in Heaven to other people on this world. Do you consider it is correct?'

'Why not?'

'It is right?'

'Of course, it is. What a silly question?'

'What types of people you are telling?'

'To the kids under 12 years of age.'

'Do they believe in you?'

'They say I am not trustworthy, Jesus Christ!'

'Are they correct?'

'I am certain they are incorrect, frankly!'

'But you still stay on this idea?'

'Yes.'

'I think you need medical support.'

'Mr Robertson, your son needs to see a brain specialist to determine his condition to be admitted to hospital or not. On my part, I need to report to local government departments on the issue. One word in advance there may be policemen coming up to bring your son to hospital if he refuses to. The period he stays in hospital will be less than 12 months, to be sure.'

'In your opinion, does he essentially go to hospital?'

'I am not able to say at this moment. On my experience it is almost certain he will. You need to wait for the specialist's report to come out. The specialist I refer to is Dr Vanesa Moore. She is an experienced doctor who has worked on this field for more than 20 years and refuses to retire.'

'Okay! Doc. I will do what you have just said. Thanks again and now we are leaving.'

'Okay! Best of luck!'

'Thanks, see you then.'

'I don't want to see you again, mate.'

'Ha, ha!'

In recent 6 or 8 months of time, Larsen is busy at home legal office doing her job. Meanwhile she takes care of Prudence who is now one year and a half. She looks like her Mum Larsen as beautiful as Larsen, honestly! God's miracle! Prudence is talking in a fluent mood on FARE Language. She listens attentively to my science tutorials in great care and interest. She always turns her face black while listening to Larsen's legal presentation. What a daughter! Prudence is glad whenever she sees a school student walks on the street. Prudence always urges to be taken to school right now. I promise her to bring her to pre-school at her age of two. She is pretty much glad at my point and now waiting anxiously to this date! What a surprise! Mum insists us to manufacture more Prudences. Mum does not mind to picking up the job to look after them before they go to school. Are we able to make another five? Don't ask me, please!

Regarding the ghost case Larsen is having a big headache. Josephine was seen pretty much in a glad mood on the day of murder. She talked to everyone in the office suite. She went to Church to pray. Afterwards Josephine told her fellow workers that she prayed for a good future of her life.

Josephine had a busy afternoon on that day. She had a conference at 1500 hours which ended at around 1619 hours. Then she hurried to the restaurant to see Ramsey. Everyone can be her witness to say she was a happy girl on that day. A couple of days before the day of murder Josephine was talking gladly to anyone she came across.

She talked everything. About her career, her marriage, her future life, her wishes and what she is going to do when she is 80 years of age. She never retires to stay to be lagging right behind her career. She always moves forward and stand up as a woman of every success. That is to stand up, stand up for Jesus!

Ramsey met Josephine every single night for 10 nights before the murder. They chatted with loud laughter where Josephine's sister all heard that. They talked for a long time which made Josephine thirsty to drink plenty of water. Josephine even joked that she would be having a wet bed in the morning. They spoke with funny jokes which made the whole apartment laughed. All of them are capable to become the witnesses. But on that night Josephine disappeared suddenly not even seeing her dead body nor the clothes she put on at that night.

Anthony who is an experienced private investigator tells Larsen there is a mysterious reason of not finding Josephine's dead body and not even her clothes. If she had died on any place, then her body should be found somewhere nearby. Alternatively, her torn pieces of clothes should be discovered on the surface of the ocean if she was drowned. It should be scattered all over the hill slopes or inside caves if she fell over the cliff. Her personal helicopter vehicle ought to be somewhere there close to the murder site. But her vehicle was standing beautifully on her vehicle park seemed to have nothing happened before. God! I hope Jesus comes back to our Earth more than once to help solve the problems. Jesus, why don't you come back earlier than expected?

In this afternoon I am hanging around inside my home office. Suddenly Prudence comes in to say she wishes to hug Grandma. Oh! God! I ask her where is Grandma whom she tells me Grandma is having a nap on that afternoon. Thus, I tell Prudence not to interrupt Grandma to let Grandma to have a leisurely break.

After the conversation, I abruptly come up with an idea. I am an advanced neurologist consultation and I am running a laboratory on my own risk. Why not to figure a method on people's conversation only with the eye contact. Hey! Is it crazy? I hope not but only fantasy. Really? Not really.

As people are capable to watch newspaper or encyclopaedia via special glasses which is put on our nostril. Why not make this splendid idea to reality? Is it? Implementing eye contacts to communicate with other organisms without saying any single word is not a smart thinking. It is done on some other Planets already. Without doubt, they can do it. Why we can't? Okay, let's do it! By what means? By all means! When it is to success? I have no idea, mate. What? Honestly, it is a difficult topic for our present scientists, mate!

As in psychology consultations which I will focus, as it is implemented by many neuroscientists currently, to emphasis on neuron functions related to emotions of humans and animals. This idea is established long time ago, but I recover it to research again.

CHAPTER 8

FRUSTRATED AND DEPRESSED

Another 15 months has elapsed but there are still no cues for the ghost case. Larsen is such frustrated that she bursts into sobbing. Not soaking! She says to herself, "Why can't I do it? Why I can't do it?" I talk to her on soft words to comfort her and to calm her down. To tell her it is not her fault. It is a matter of time to solve the blocks.

In these few days her mood becomes better. I ask her when is the right time which she wishes to have a second pregnancy. She tells me,

'I will become pregnant again after the case.'

'What did you say?'

'I will be having another baby as soon as the case is completed, honestly.'

'That means I need to wait for a couple of months.'

'That's correct.'

'If the case is not solved for another 10 or 15 years. Then I will ......'

'That's right. You will have to wait for 10 years.'

'Oh! My God!'

'God can help you whenever you pray to Him, to be honest!'

'Jesus, why don't you come back for a second time?'

'Jesus will help you!'

'Do you have any cues now?'

'Not really!'

'That means what?'

'That means you are on the waiting list!'

'Lord!'

'Ask for Buddha's mercy, darling!'

'We will enjoy sex now!'

'Oh! No. You bustard!'

'Come on baby, let's do it!'

'Oh! Funking! ………. Funking you! ………….'

'I am happy!'

'Oh! My God! Help!'

'God is coming to help you, sweetie!'

'Forgive me, forgive me. Oh! Help! Please ……… help!'

Prudence is ready to go to pre-school now. She is pretty much excited and enjoyable to study to learn new knowledge. After school what she does is holding a book to read and read without stop. She sits there for hours without moving and no drowsiness. God! Is she alright?

Regarding the ghost case which Larsen is having a headache. On second thought! If Josephine was killed on that night. There should have at least one person saw it or heard Josephine's cry for help. There is no witness on hand. No matter where Josephine had flown to. Her vehicle ought to have a record on Specific Signals System or SSS. This device was once called the black box on civil aeroplanes at ancient time. It is now upgraded to be known as Triple-S.

Josephine's helicopter vehicle is parked on the parking spot same as Josephine has parked it there every night when she is home after her work. If it was parked by someone else. Would it be Ramsey? Ramsey was together with Josephine all night long on the night of event. Everyone noticed it. If it was Ramsey. Then what means he implemented? What the Triple-S has recorded is where Josephine had flown to and the time she flew back to home, nothing else! God, please help me, please. It is my answer to the puzzle!

Recently Larsen does not look happy as usual. In these weeks she looks worry and upset. Prudence is now going to pre-school. Prudence becomes a happy girl suddenly.

At the time of 2118 hours. Mum is fatigue and is sound asleep inside her bedroom after talking with us the whole evening. Tonight, I am quite tired and ready to go to sleep. Larsen discuss the ghost case with me. I advise her to directly go to see Josephine's family to initiate to take up this ghost case. By that time the whole party is capable to work collaborate on this issue.

'Baby, shall we have sex now?'

'God, what's the matter with you?'

'You have no mood at this time, do you?'

'I am pretty much fatigue, darling! Sorry Love!'

'Let's do it in the morning, then. Okay?'

'Fine!'

In the morning Mum is getting up early but sometimes goes back to sleep for another one or two hours. During this period, Larsen chat with me while Larsen is at home to discuss the home matters. In the afternoon Mum is watching Cyber TV or reading news or story books via her Computer Glasses. At night the whole family is having dinner and a happy chat time.

It is now close to lunch time. Prudence should be home after her first month in pre-school. I am waiting anxiously while worrying would there be any accidents happened as Prudence is late at this time? Suddenly the door TV appears Prudence's face. I therefore, hurry to open the door by pressing the button.

'Hi, Dad. What's lunch today?'

'There is no lunch today.'

'Why is it?'

'You are pretty much late, and we already had our lunch. Darling!'

'Any food left, please?'

'There is only some soup and a piece of lion-elephant meat remaining.'

'Only these, Dad?'

'Yes, only these.'

'I will take all, honestly!'

'Enjoy your lunch!'

After 10 minutes, Prudence asks me,

'Please Dad, may I have some more?'

'What?'

'Yeah! Some more please!'

'Are you crazy, Prudence?'

'I am starving!'

'Okay, I cook some fish pancakes for you. Okay?'

'Yes, please!'

After the lunch, Prudence is playing her kid-computer on her plain brown transitional glasses. I watch her for a while and notice she seems watching or reading something interesting or exciting.

'What are you doing, Prudence?'

'I am watching this morning's class collaborate session.'

'Really?'

'Of course, what a silly question!'

'What did you do this morning?'

'The teacher taught us to sing a song.'

'Which song?'

'The Flying Bird.'

'Really?'

'Absolutely!'

'Are you able to sing it to me now?'

'Sorry, Dad. I can't!'

'What's the matter?'

'I don't know the song.'

'Why?'

'While I am learning the song. I always forget the lyrics but other students keep singing which I can't follow.'

'Then?'

'Then what?'

'What happened?'

'I only open my mouth pretending singing aloud to deceive the music teacher.'

'Did she realise you are left behind?'

'Of course not. She kept urging us to sing. Then we were singing faster and faster and then it was time to be home.'

'That's perfect, Prudence! Absolutely perfect!'

'Before this, I am looking to become a Galaxy singer, song writer and album producer.'

'Now?'

'Now, it's all gone.'

'Oh! What a day!'

'It's not a day or sunny day. It is a rainy day. Oh, my God!'

'What else do you usually do in school?'

'Once, it is recess time. I am happy and walk out of my student motor vehicle to have a look of other students in the playground.'

'What then?'

'As soon as I am in the corridor. Suddenly, someone collides on me and I have sensory troubles.'

'What happens?'

'I immediately tell myself to say something to find out I can hear what I have just said or not.'

'Then, I succeed.'

'Good girl!'

'Exactly!'

'Who was that student?'

'I have no idea! He disappeared as fast as a morning dew. I could see him nowhere.'

'Alright! Enjoy what you were doing. I am going on my research. Okay?'

'Okay, Dad!'

'Not Dad. It is Papa. Not dead.'

Regarding my research, I wish to find out a means for people to talk without opening their mouth. That is to read the other people's mind! Can I do it? No idea! It is supposed to happen in ancient science fantasy movies that people on other planets are capable to talk via brain signals. This is exactly happening on Galaxy A219. Those people, we call them people just like we humans, but they are not supposed to be named as people or simply not humans or we say they are half-human and half-animal or simply humal-hybrid. A better name for them.

What is their method of communicating? I am sure God will understand! To talk and exchange signals without any movements of the body nor sound of words is a difficult task for us even after the 53rd century on Planet Earth in our Milky Galaxy, honestly! This way of conversing is tricky and non-understandable by Earth Scientists through the previous 52 centuries or may be not happened on the Island of Atlantis at that time of the year, mate!

Regarding the Island of Atlantis which is a mysterious island with high civilisations on Earth and to have contact with outside Planets which they visit us, or we go to see them as friends. There is no mention of any war nor battle fighting at that time. Do you believe in this? I can't believe it! Don't believe it then!

The Island was sunk to the bottom of the sea may be because of earthquake, eruption or by other natural disasters. Who knows? These natural disasters are potent that no one can imagine its power and ability and its destructive mechanisms throughout our human history up to this time of the year! We are still wondering what is happening inside our earth crust which the roaring fire is hurrying to burst on the land where we are residing currently. Do you wish this to happen? Don't ask me! I don't know!

There are some Galaxies with hundreds of light years apart from Milky Galaxy where they have dictators or Emperors ruling their whole Galaxy. These places are almost exactly like the Planet Earth before the 15th century with autocrats commanding the whole kingdom. These are backward civilisations which will certainly disappear in the future which is much more similar as the present Earth. Some may stay as Federation as FACE or other bureaucratic form of Galaxy Governments looks like current situations. No matter what. These are all God's schedule which humans have no decisive vote but God, frankly! Who knows?

Today is Saturday with a lovely cloudy weather. No strong and hot sunlight but only gusts with a chilly emotion on everyone. Mum is such happy that the whole family goes out to a museum to see artefacts in Galaxy Wars in century 28. We also are planning to watch the documentary film inside the museum micro-cam hall on what the soldiers' stress disorder was affecting them at that time and under what type of health care conditions.

We are talking happily while waiting for the flying-bus and Prudence is screaming and eagerly to look for a boyfriend. What's the matter of you?

While staying inside the Galaxy V South-Territory Museum with a hungry attitude. We go into a burger shop to eat those edibles. We are starving!

In the cam hall where I am purchasing the tickets via the video ticket machine. Prudence says suddenly that she has found her love. Oh! Jesus Christ! At such an age! When we are watching the documentary film. Mum says these are inhuman behaviours and non-sense and stupidity. There are many audiences watching and the hall is crowded with every single type of organisms. They come from different Galaxies including our Planet Earth. While walking out to catch a flying bus ready to return home. Larsen is collapsed and falls to my arms. Lord!

In the hospital where Mum is anxious to know the reason why. We are all waiting at the waiting room. Then, here comes the doctor. What the doctor is telling us will be Larsen is pregnant. Mum is such happy that she bursts out with tears. It is a surprise shock to me because I will be father again! Lord!

Two days later in my home psychology clinic where I am waiting for my client to come back for another consultation. I am pretty much sleepy that I nearly fall asleep. Around this time episode in the afternoon on Wednesday week my client suddenly turns up.

'Good afternoon, Doctor. Good to see you again!'

'It's nice to see you, Pedro. Sit down please.'

'Thank, doc.'

'Referring to your previous couple of consultations which you tell me your friends do not talk to you and even not playing with you. Is that correct?'

'Absolutely!'

'You are feeling nothing unusual up to this moment. Is that correct?'

'Exactly!'

'They say you are arrogant and despise on other people.'

'Definitely!'

'You also tell me you keep doing what you are doing as usual.'

'Of course, I am.'

'What's your purpose to see a psychologist then?'

'I wish to find out what I have done wrong and what I am going to do in the future.'

'You have done nothing wrong, mate.'

'Why they hate me at such a horrible degree?'

'You say that they consider you are a mean person.'

'I think so!'

'What does that mean, Pedro?'

'They defame my reputation and ignore my existence.'

'Now, Pedro. Don't let yourself as the most vital person in the Milky Galaxy.'

'Is it?'

'Do whatever you like to do.'

'Then?'

'What are you doing now?'

'I am working as a working director in an astro-machinery engineering firm in south-west of this suburb.'

'Go on.'

'Do you think I need friends?'

'No matter what you do. There is person says you are correct and some say you are wrong.'

'I don't mind!'

'You need friends but not many. To find a good friend is not an easy stuff, honestly.'

'Your recommendation?'

'Besides work what else are you doing?'

'Hanging around.'

'Whenever you think fit. Just keep doing it. Don't bother what other people are saying. You don't need to make them happy but your spouse.'

'I think what I have done are correct.'

'It needs to wait for God's Final Judgement Day.'

'At that time........?'

'At that time all people know you are correct or not correct.'

'I think ....'

'You just keep doing what you are doing. Don't listen to others' complaints and defamation. It is no good to you.'

'Have I done something wrong?'

'This is the reason you come to see a psychologist.'

'Why?'

'It all concerns with your emotion.'

'Psychologically unbalance?'

'Pretty much!'

'What's wrong with that, Doc?'

'This is psychology, Pedro.'

'What psychology?'

'You must stay in gladness and look to the bright side of the Galaxy. Otherwise you are in deep trouble.'

'I have no trouble, to be certain.'

'What's your worry, then?'

'Not much worry!'

'You are capable to do anything on your own.'

'Nowadays all work is done in collaboration.'

'Look at the scientists.'

'What?'

'They figure out a theory from their observation.'

'Then?'

'Then they figure experiments to test the hypothesis.'

'Then?'

'Then they either work by themselves or work with other scientists to find out the truth.'

'I think ....'

'I think you are capable to do anything. Only on occasions when you need to do it on your own.'

'You mean I can work on my own and with others?'

'Of course. Why not?'

'Some jealous at my merits.'

'I tell you a true story.

'There is a guy who went to a new migrated country. At that time the people in the migrated country hate him as an alien.'

'Why?'

'After that person who is a scientist who make an advanced scientific innovation to bring up the country's status on World Science and Political stage. Everybody loves him.'

'Why?'

'It's all about emotion.'

'What then?'

'Whenever you are good to a person. Then that person will be good to you in return.'

'I think ....'

'Of course, some people are still jealous. But don't bother.'

'What should I do then?'

'Do what you think fit and ignore others' accusation.'

'Only these?'

'This consultation is a final one and I charge you double the fee as we have a detailed discussion to clear all your puzzles.'

'I will pay.'

'Thanks very much and I don't want to see you again.'

'Bye Doc.'

'See you!'

Another five days have elapsed. Larsen is talking with investigator Anthony inside her office.

'Any new threads to be found?'

'None.'

'Any good news.'

'Not now.'

'We need to have a detailed discussion today, Anthony.'

'Of course, why not!'

'First, we need to work out what Ramsey is doing around the night of murder.'

'I have asked his friends.'

'What?'

'They all say he is doing fine on those days. Nothing unusual.'

'The same?'

'Exactly the same.'

'Does Ramsey say or do anything that is suspicious?'

'They all say no.'

'He has a lot of friends actually, right?'

'Not really!'

'What is the number?'

'He has only two friends.'

'What are the two friends doing?'

'One works in an always-new-machines making as senior engineering officer. The other one is a Lecturer of Galaxy History on Civilisations.'

'They don't look like suspects, do they?'

'I also found out that both guys have good reputation in their social sphere.'

'What Ramsey is doing in those days?'

'He is busy to go all around the country to see clients and business conferences.'

'All the time?'

'Every day.'

'No breaks?'

'Even at the weekends.'

'Superman, right?'

'May be.'

'Has he visited any ammunition vendors or other firearms firms by himself secretly?'

'No one mentions that.'

'By your experience, what can you figure out?'

'It is a headache without any cues and no witnesses. It is my first tricky case honestly.'

'That means no clues.'

'Yes, no hints.'

'Go home then.

'Okay! Bye.'

'See you later!'

On this day Larsen is pretty much in glad mood. She says to me she is having a baby boy which is told by her Medical Specialist Ross. Larsen prefers the boy is called Hayden Salvator and asks my comments.

Of course, I need to say 'Yes'. Why not? Jesus! The boy's nicked name is Makiah.

Prudence comes along to talk to me. What she is saying is her nonsense. Prudence tells me her teacher caretaker tells the class of 15 children to memorise a passage from the essay given by that teacher. Not any singular passage on the essay is assigned to them and the children themselves are permitted to choose for their own. The next day the teacher Margaret will ask some of them to tell their own passage to speak to the whole class.

What Prudence is telling me which is, she forgets the whole matter. The next day she attends class and is worried while Margaret is calling children to stand up for the speech. Unfortunately, Prudence is saved and no problem.

The second time, this happens again. Unfortunately, Prudence is saved again. Excuse me! Prudence is such a happy girl who thinks everything is fine and everyone is alright. Lord! What can or what should I do? She is on her lucky days which she is still a young girl and does not understand the burdens on study and career! Jesus Christ Superstar!

'Hi, Doc!'

'Hi, Smith.'

'Doc, shall we continue?'

'Of course, why not?'

'Where was I?'

'The couple of consultations recently, you keep on saying and insist someone stole your thesis as her own. Right?'

'Yes, she is.'

'Her name is Joanna. Correct?'

'Absolutely.'

'Joanna steals your thesis.'

'Right.'

'On the contrary, you also have submitted the same thesis to your Professor. Right?'

'Right you are.'

'What have the Professor told you?'

'He says nothing.'

'What grade do you get?'

'High Distinction.'

'What about Joanna?'

'She says it is Credit.'

'Then nothing happens?'

'Yeah! Nothing happens. Fortunately!'

'What evidence to support what you are saying?'

'I think she has done that.'

'You think?'

'Of course. What's wrong of it?'

'You think. Everything you think is always right?'

'Of course! What a genius!'

'Do you understand?'

'Understand what?'

'Are you telling me the truth?'

'I am, to be sure. Why?'

'Do you ask the Professor on the thesis Joanna submitted?'

'What for?'

'To find out is her thesis containing some information on your own thesis.'

'Non-sense!'

'What is non-sense?'

'It is ridiculous!'

'What?'

'I am certain she has stolen my thesis, Doc.'

'Really certain?'

'Sure!'

'What can you prove to me?'

'I have an idea she does it?'

'What idea?'

'A splendid idea, mate!'

'You think she does. You do not ask your Professor for evidence. You insist to say she does. You do not have a look at her thesis. From all of these that you conclude she steals your thesis. Right?'

'Right you are!'

'I think you are on the right track! Mate.'

'What track?'

'The tricky track.'

'What?'

'You cannot confirm a person who has done something by what you are thinking of that person.'

'What?'

'You need to collect evidence.'

'Why?'

'It is learnt from your study.'

'I do.'

'Then what have you done.'

'I have done a wrong task.'

'Sure?'

'Pretty sure!'

'Okay, you do not need to come back on condition you do not have all these unacceptable thinking to happen again.'

'Thanks, Doc.'

'Okay, bye.'

'Thanks, Doc.'

CHAPTER 9

WHAT A CASE

egarding the ghost case, it is understood the case is a dirty and cunny one, without doubt!

Larsen asks Anthony,

'Do you get new clues?'

'Probably and honestly.'

'What's that?'

'It is found that Ramsey went to Planet UQZ5 after he was graduated.'

'What followed?'

'He tells his friends when he came back to FARE while he was there he saw an ancient Roman god, Dea Tacita.'

'And?'

'The Roman god told him to go to a hillside where he would meet a person. That person will help him on whateverhe is doing.'

'What's the type of god Dea Tacita?'

'She is the "The Silent Goddess". A goddess of dead.'

'Did Ramsey go there?'

'Yes. From then on, he always tells people to worship Dea Tacita. Just like our priests and Holy Father tells us to worship our Lord God.'

'There's difference.'

'Of course, there is.'

'What do you think?'

'Dea Tacita is not a good goddess. She manages the dead.'

'The priests?'

'They urge people to do the right thing. That's the difference!'

'Absolutely correct!'

'What can I say then?'

'Who is the friend?'

'He is the man working on Technology Development in a large organisation on the Planet.'

'What's his name?'

'He is called Dimaroo.'

'What is he doing now?'

'He is working in a corporation manufacturing new machines which are ordered by customers.'

'Any other friends?'

'There is one more friend, but it is very difficult to trace where he is.'

'Why?'

'I don't know why!'

'On the same Planet?'

'Yes, for sure!'

'Does Ramsey contact Damaroo?'

'Yeah! They keep on sending trans-galaxy t-mails very often.'

'Any more cues?'

'No.'

'I want you to track down what communication contents are Ramsey and Damaroo exchanging. Also, I wish you to ask your assistant Beth to seduce Ramsey. From then we are capable to obtain first-hand information on what Ramsey is doing. Okay?'

'There is no hope on this from my experience, actually!'

'This is the hope of among hopelessness. You can ask Pope for advice if you want to.'

'What can Beth do honestly?'

'Tell Beth to get close to Ramsey to find out what he is doing and report to us.'

'It is very dangerous!'

'Find one more partner to help Beth which they both work together in case something goes wrong.'

'Got it!'

'By the way do you think Ramsey did see Dea Tacita on that Planet?'

'It is told by Ramsey himself.'

'Ramsey is a big liar!'

'He definitely is.'

'Do you think he can be trusted on this matter?'

'Hopefully!'

'Really?'

'What am I able to say?'

After Anthony has left. Larsen is in deep thought.....

What can Damaroo do if he did help Ramsey in the murder case. Damaroo is only a poor worker in a corporation. He can do nothing, can't he? The Planet where he lives is a backward society where there are eruptions and tsunami all year round. Every time in the fourteenth month of their calendar there is certain many flooding on the whole Planet which the authority needs outside aids.

What about the other guy? We do not know his name. We do not know where he is. We do not know what he is doing, his career and education and family background. We even do not know there is such a person or not! Who is this person?

Regarding Josephine's sister Maggie who holds a high position in an archaeology firm in one of the high commercial buildings in Central Business District. Her Boss is a busy man keen on earning money. It is why his working staffs are always sent to other Planets to research the former Dynasty's ruined Palaces, buildings and the archaeology structure and the utensils which were manufactured at that time to be documented and air on different Planet TV Cinemas. He, Robert earns a big profit which explains of his big spending and his children's expensive travelling journeys from here to there.

Robert is a loyal husband but does not care of his offspring such that the children go out to play all the time and not pay much attention on their college assessments which aroused Robert's fierce annoyance and ends up in big quarrel that disturbs the family harmony every now and then. His wife, Belinda says nothing and that's it!

Maggie is busy only in the mornings with conference almost every morning held for two hours or may be longer. In the afternoon Maggie sits on her boss chair with left palm on her cheek looking at fellow colleagues busily doing their job outside her office suite. She has a light lunch. Hence, she does not put on weight but already gets a big waist and goes to lose weight in fitness gymnasium on Tuesdays and Fridays before going home. What a week!

On Ramsey's issue there are many evidences to support that he is a playboy. Every time after party he will for certain, to make love with a girl in the party. Anthony discovers that Ramsey has a secret daughter outside who not even Josephine knows. It is Ramsey's top secret.

It is why Ramsey has infected by Sexual Transmitted Disease.

Although it does not affect Ramsey's body health due to modern medical achievements. It really hurts his own daughter who died on STD at the age of 7. This brief account is disclosed by the doctor who took care of Ramsey's daughter's final months.

Jesus, what are you doing? It is a good job, isn't it? What about others? Christ! For God's mercy and Lord's sympathy! This news is not known to anybody and Ramsey does not feel upset nor unhappy. He is glad that his daughter is dead because his daughter is a hinderance to Ramsey's future career to marry a wealthy girl and goes into upper class in society. Almighty God! What is he expecting? A comfort or relaxation or just get over it? What a mean!

By the way what is Ramsey planning to do now? God knows! Don't ask me! Ask another person who is capable to give you some cues. Okay?

Okay! Got it!

Beth and the other girl, Roberta finds out Ramsey is addicted on opium cancer-causing drinks which Ramsey drinks in the morning before he goes out. Whenever he does not then he is irritated, and vision impaired with blurred eyes and an unsteady walking pace. This is a good record because at least we understand why Ramsey expends a large lump sum every month that we have no indication where the money has gone to.

What is Ramsey doing now? No one knows! Unfortunately, Anthony meets a young girl age 22 named Dorothy with naked name called Pussy Lion. She is an architect somewhere on a place where in ancient history is called Europe and then now called Continent 1 on FACE.

Dorothy is now engaged with fiancé Christopher leading a lovable life together. Before their engagement there is something happened. This is Dorothy's story,

At that time when I am a university undergraduate in engineering major in aircraft design. On one night which happens suddenly that I meet Ramsey in my friend's wedding party. After the very party I am heading to go home. Ramsey seduces and forcefully or close to the crime to rape me. I strangle by what I have learned from Martial Arts to a point he is nearly dead. He begs me by saying he loves me from the first exchange of eye contact during the birthday party. He tells me that he loves me such as Romeo. At that time episode I have some pity on him and let him go.

After this incidence that Ramsey comes back to revenge. Ramsey knows Chris is a social science undergraduate major in social development and design. Chris has to make an effort to go all over FARE to research and gain a clear understanding of those social formation of modern and ancient communities all around.

Ramsey lies to me by saying Chris has two mistresses on the other part of FARE and has many girlfriends everywhere. Christopher is a playboy. Ramsey says in an empathy mood as he knows my hurt feeling and with his beautiful planned story to conceive. I nearly fall into his trap. At first, I am in puzzle wondering why Chris would do such a matter to me which I know deeply that Chris loves me from the bottom of his heart.

Ramsey keeps saying such lie to me in the following few months and every time there is new cheated evidence supplied by Ramsey to deceive myself. Ramsey knows a friend of Christopher whom tells Ramsey about Christopher's daily life in drinking lots of whisky in a pub.

What I later have found is that Chris stays in residential places wherever he goes without going out late at night. From all people who knows Ramsey tell me Ramsey seldom talks in public since he is not good at arguing with other guys. From my observations and my understandings, I reckon Chris is not pretending as what Ramsey says. Chris always states his idea which is proved to be universal truth in debates and contests in front of a huge crowd and Chris does not scare anyone who may beat him because Chris has his confidence.

From what Dorothy has said Larsen is pretty sure Ramsey should prepare to jail for the rest of his life on verdict of 999 years long as there is no death penalty any more on FACE.

Some days later our baby boy is born with a large head and muscles all over his body. Then on Thursday afternoon Larsen receives a call from Maggie who formally invites Larsen to represent Maggie on the case to sue Ramsey on murdering Josephine. Larsen is such a happy girl that she disturbs me all night on telling me about her feeling, gladness and why she is certain to bring Ramsey to jail. On Friday I am not able to go to Lab and stays home idling to hang around. Jesus Christ!

After dinner, Larsen is in deep thought:

"If Ramsey is the murderer then where is Josephine's dead body? By what means does Ramsey kill Josephine? Ramsey has not got many friends. Does he need a helping hand to commit the crime? No one knows indeed!

"If Ramsey needs aids from outside. Where is the aid? A friend or any person? Ramsey's friends are all look like good gentlemen without any cheating behaviour nor character. Whenever a friend helps Ramsey. Who is this guy? Does Ramsey have other friends that we do not know? If 'Yes'. Who is he and where is he now? What method do they communicate? Not emails. Ramsey's emails and any other people's emails are under surveillance and checked by government. There is no record of communication.

"Is Josephine really died? If "No". Where is she? She hides in a cave or in a friend's house? Or she is still struggling to survive in a place without human inhabitation? If "Yes". Where is her dead body? There is no hints of any flesh nor torn clothes worn by Josephine on the night of murder that is left somewhere else to be found by constables nor us. Such that the pieces can be tested by DNA technology.

"It should be correct to say Josephine is not on this Planet. Is she flown to other Planets? Is she still living on our Earth Planet? Where is Josephine?

"There is an ancient magic performed on a small area somewhere on Earth in the 18th century. The witches could call a spirit back to life and listen to the witch's order. This type of old magicians, were out of sight currently. There is none left at this moment.

"The dream I got some time ago is the ghost or spirit recalled by magician? No one knows all these dirty magics nowadays, do we? If Josephine is still alive. Who is the ghost in my dream? My imagination or fantasy?"

'Honey, what are you doing?'

'I am trying to work out a suitable solution to the ghost case.'

'Really?'

'Perfectly!'

'What are you doing now?' Larsen asks me.

'On what?'

'On your science projects.'

'Oh! I … eh …… I am sending a Space Ship to a Black Hole ……. Eh …… at the …… eh …….'

'What?'

'At the other end of our Milky Galaxy.'

'A large project!'

'Yeah, a large one.'

'When?'

'As soon as possible, Baby.'

'Good idea.'

'Exactly!'

'What's the purpose?'

'To explore the origin of Human species.'

'By what means?'

'The Ship is to move into the Black Hole slowly and quietly.'

'Then?'

'Then, it will retreat backwards a bit and forward again.'

'Why?'

'To offset the pressure inside the Black Hole.'

'And?'

'It will move a little bit forward and then a little bit forward until it reaches the other end.'

'Why?'

'To explore our species is from that area originated in our ancient time.'

'Why is that?'

'At that position which may have obstacles there.'

'Then?'

'The Ship is armed with Laser beam.'

'What?'

'It is to fire at the target whenever essential.'

'Good point, Darling.'

'Yeah! Absolutely.'

'When are you sending the Space Ship?'

'Early next week as scheduled.'

'Good luck, Darling.'

'Thanks, Sweetie.'

'Okay! Good night.'

'Enjoy a good sound asleep!'

'Yes, I will.'
'Good night!'

Prudence is busy on her legal research. She says she will learn from Larsen to become a Barrister one day. Such that Prudence is capable to argue with other lawyers and cross-examine witnesses. This is what she thinks. Will she one day become a lawyer? Who knows! Don't ask me. Ask someone who knows, please. While her younger brother is having a nap after lunch. Oh! It is 1:30pm I must hurry to my lab.

Regarding Larsen's ghost case, there is no big step to move forward. Anthony is always discussing with Beth to figure any thread from anywhere at any time from onset of the night of murder up to present moment. No Luck! Jesus, I hope you are coming back the second time!

If Josephine is dead. Where did she die? Where is her body now? There will be some cues by now. But it isn't. Goodness me! If Josephine is still alive. Where is she and what method does she use to survive? If she can survive, where is she hiding from, who supports her livings, and can she contact her family again? Anthony is in depression which he invites Rebecca to go out for a walk. This is a long walk!

Now it is half past nine in the morning. I am hanging around inside my home clinic for 15 minutes, nothing to do! God! Suddenly, the video-phone is making its scream. It is Larsen. She tells me there is good news on the ghost mystery. She will tell the family while she is back home. She promises. Lord! Is it good news indeed? Whenever it turns out to become nasty. What's going to happen? Lord!

On neuroscience field, there is mystery on human brain functions. By this century much is resolved but what makes a new life to come to this world is still a mystery. God makes us! God's miracle! Many parts of human brain are seemed to be understood. Where is the large picture?

What means do the brain functions well in healthy body and bad in patients? It needs a second thought, mate!

In the Law Court,

'Mr Ramsey, on the night when Josephine disappeared, where were you?'

'I stayed with her on dinner and went to a Park to have some fresh air.'

'After that?'

'I saw her driving her helicopter vehicle back home.'

'Was she going home?'

'She told me "Yes".'

'Then where were you?'

'I went home.'

'After that?'

'I went to sleep.'

'Did you see Josephine afterwards?'

'Not really!'

'Why?'

'I have no idea. I call her without any response.'

'Why does she suddenly disappear?'

'Don't ask me. Ask the police!'

'In these 5 years of time did you pursue other girls?'

'No! Of course not!'

'Really?'

'Of course, why I pursue other girls?'

'It is because you have already killed Josephine. Is that correct?'

'No, definitely no!'

'Where is Josephine now?'

'What can I say? What can I tell? We lost contact in such a long period. I have no idea where she is now.'

'What are you doing now?'

'I work in my office to do my job and now you are cross-examining me in Court.'

'Really?'

'Are you asking me questions right now?'

'I am telling you right now. You have killed Josephine. Have you not?'

'No!'

'Why Josephine is completely vanished?'

'If Josephine is dead. Where is her dead body?'

'.....................'

'Where is her dead body now?'

'.................'

'Answer me, Barrister!'

'I have no idea at this stage.'

'Where is Josephine right now?'

'................'

After a couple of public holidays. The court resumed. In these few days Larsen is very fatigue and no smiling face. I try to comfort her, but she always says she is fine and not even eat any meat or fish during meals. She only takes in cereals and coffee. That's it. God!

In Court Room,

'Mr Ramsey, you told the court that you have not killed Josephine. Is it correct?'

'Of course, I didn't.'

'What was the weather on the murder night?'

'It was hot such that I have got lots of sweat on my face and my clothes.'

'Why the weather was hot at that time?'

'It was Spring or mid-Spring. The wind was a hot mass from the west. Everyone was complaining but no one has figured a solution.'

'Indeed!'

'Yes, indeed!'

'It is because Josephine was dropped into the ocean and is eaten by a whale or bear which has been hungry after a long cold and starving Winter. Especially they have to feed their cubs.'

'Why did you say this?'

'It was you and your partner scheduled this plot to murder Josephine.'

'I have no partner, Barrister!'

'Your partner is named Stuart.'

'No, I have no friend called Stuart!'

'Actually, Stuart is a friend you have known not a long time ago. Stuart is good at Roman gods and Greek gods and the myths.'

'What myths?'

'He tells you many matters about those gods' good and bad attitudes towards humans.'

'What?'

'He also informs you on what to avoid or escape from their punishments.'

'Why?'

'It was Stuart who begged these gods to a conspiracy on what way to kill Josephine would be in a perfect and unknown murder schedule.'

'No, he didn't tell me!'

'It means you actually have a friend called Stuart, haven't you, Mr Ramsey?'

'................'

'Objection. It is totally irrelevant!' Defence Barrister says.

'Your Honour, I have sufficient evidences to prove what I have said.'

'Okay!'

'Mr Ramsey, it is you to put in PPHOD powder in Josephine's drinks to cause her drowsiness and unconsciousness.'

'No, I didn't!'

'Yes, you did.'

'Why I did it?'

'To kill Josephine and then go to marry a wealthy girl. Am I correct?'

'No, you are not!'

'Of course! Everyone is expecting you will say I am not correct. It is your pretext, isn't it?'

'No, you are making up stories.'

'Where is Josephine's body now, Mr Ramsey?'

'She is having a break at my residence.'

'What?'

'Yes, I found her in the public holidays and she is fine.'

'What?'

After a couple of Court sessions,

'Miss Josephine, you told the court you were living alone in an island surrounded by sea. Is it right?'

'Yes, you are right.'

'What is the length of time?'

'More than 5 years and going to be 6 years long.'

'What method to keep you alive?'

'I ate fish from the sea after they were grilled.'

'What was the number of fishes you ate a meal or a day?'

'More than 5 fishes per day.'

'You still love to eat fish, don't you?'

'Yes, of course!'

'Now Miss Josephine right here is a grilled fish. Please eat it straight away!'

'No, I won't.'

'Why you won't?'

'I ate too many on the island!'

'You just told the Court you still like to eat grilled fish, haven't you, Miss Josephine?'

'Yes,....... But ...... but ....'

'But what?'

'It is disgusting!'

'Please tell the Court why it is disgusting, Miss Josephine?'

'.............'

'Eat it!'

'No!'

'Eat it!'

'No!'

'You do not eat this grilled fish is totally because you are not Josephine.'

'Why only Josephine eats fish?'

'It is because you are a robot!'

'No, I am not a robot.'

'All evidences provided by you in Court are inside your memory sim card inserted by Ramsey. Thus, you know everything about Josephine and your body figure is created same as Josephine. The only difference is you are made of latest soft steel as similar as to human skin.'

'No, you are not correct!'

'Whenever I am wrong. Why don't you eat the fish then?'

'..........'

Two months later the verdict to Ramsey is to be jailed for 257 years with a minimum of 120 years in jail. It is because there is no death penalty on FACE any more. Josephine's family members and friends are not satisfied as Ramsey is a cold-blooded killer. Ramsey deserved to be cut to slices to feed the tigers.

In these days I am able to see Larsen to have a smiling face again and she is talking and talking gladly ever.

Printed in the United States
By Bookmasters